The Tiara Club

at Silver Towers

For Princess Kanuja
VF

www.tiaraclub.co.uk

ORCHARD BOOKS
338 Euston Road, London NW1 3BH
Orchard Books Australia
Level 17/207 Kent Street, Sydney, NSW 2000
A Paperback Original
First published by Orchard Books as individual editions in 2006
This 2-in-1 edition published 2009
Text © Vivian French 2006
Illustrations © Sarah Gibb 2006
The rights of Vivian French and Sarah Gibb to be identified as the author
and illustrator of this work have been asserted by them in accordance
with the Copyright, Designs and Patents Act, 1988.

A CIP catalogue record for this book is available from the British Library.
ISBN 978 1 40830 676 5
3 5 7 9 10 8 6 4 2

Printed in Great Britain
Orchard Books is a division of Hachette Children's Books,
an Hachette UK company.
www.hachette.co.uk

The Tiara Club

at Silver Towers

Daisy & Alice at Silver Towers

By Vivian French

Illustrated by Sarah Gibb

ORCHARD BOOKS

The Royal Palace Academy
for the Preparation of Perfect Princesses

(Known to our students as "*The Princess Academy*")

OUR SCHOOL MOTTO:
A Perfect Princess always thinks of others
before herself, and is kind, caring and truthful.

Silver Towers offers a complete education for
Tiara Club princesses with emphasis on selected
outings. The curriculum includes:

Fans and Curtseys	*Problem Prime Ministers*
A visit to Witch Windlespin	*A visit to the Museum of Royal Life*
(Royal herbalist, healer and maker of magic potions)	*(Students will be well protected from the Poisoned Apple)*

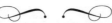

Our headteacher, Queen Samantha Joy, is present
at all times, and students are well looked after
by the school Fairy Godmother, Fairy Angora.

Our resident staff and visiting experts include:

LADY ALBINA MacSPLINTER (School Secretary)	*QUEEN MOTHER MATILDA* (Etiquette, Posture and Poise)
CROWN PRINCE DANDINO (School Excursions)	*FAIRY G* (Head Fairy Godmother)

We award tiara points to encourage our Tiara Club princesses towards the next level. All princesses who win enough points at Silver Towers will attend the Silver Ball, where they will be presented with their Silver Sashes.

Silver Sash Tiara Club princesses are invited to return to Ruby Mansions, our exclusive residence for Perfect Princesses, where they may continue their education at a higher level.

PLEASE NOTE:
Princesses are expected to arrive at the Academy with a *minimum* of:

TWENTY BALL GOWNS
(with all necessary hoops, petticoats, etc)

TWELVE DAY DRESSES

SEVEN GOWNS
suitable for garden parties, and other special day occasions

TWELVE TIARAS

DANCING SHOES
five pairs

VELVET SLIPPERS
three pairs

RIDING BOOTS
two pairs

Cloaks, muffs, stoles, gloves and other essential accessories as required

The Tiara Club
at Silver Towers

Princess Daisy
and the Magical Merry-Go-Round

By Vivian French
Illustrated by Sarah Gibb

ORCHARD BOOKS

Hello! I'm Daisy. Princess Daisy.
And I do hope you're enjoying being
at Silver Towers with us. You're exactly
the right kind of princess, you
know – just like my lovely friends,
Charlotte, Katie, Alice, Sophia and Emily.
And not at all like Diamonde and
Gruella – they're SO big-headed.
Do you get nervous before you do
something new? I do – I try SO hard
not to, but I can't help it. And learning
to be a Perfect Princess means
we're ALWAYS doing new things,
or going to new places...

Chapter One

We were sitting in the Homework Room when Princess Freya came ZOOMING in.

"Have any of you seen the noticeboard?" she gasped. "There's a garden fair on Saturday, and a Flower Petal Ball afterwards! Can't stop – got to tell everyone – byeee!" and she was gone.

We stared at each other for a moment, and then Charlotte snatched up her books.

"Quick!" she said. "Let's go and have a look!" The noticeboard is outside the breakfast hall, and if there are any school events or invitations Lady Albina pins them up. We're expected to check the board regularly – but we aren't always very good at remembering!

Anyway, we hurtled down the stairs, but we weren't the first there – LOADS of princesses were staring at the HUGE invitation pinned to the board.

YOU ARE ALL INVITED
TO KING PERCIVAL'S
ROYAL GARDEN FAIR!

This Saturday.

3.00pm until late.

Listen to the Royal Brass Band!

Wander in the flower gardens!

Row on the lake!

Ride on the Marvellous Merry-Go-Round!

NB The day will end with
a Flower Petal Ball

"Wow!" said Charlotte. "That sounds SO brilliant! And it's Saturday tomorrow!"

Alice's eyes were shining. "I ADORE merry-go-rounds," she said. "Let's all have a go together, and we can whirl round and round and ROUND!"

"YES!" Emily and Katie sounded just as thrilled as Alice.

"Merry-go-rounds are the BEST!" Sophia said. "What do you think, Daisy?"

"Yes," I said, "it'll be fun." And I hoped I sounded as if I really truly meant it.

Does that sound odd? The trouble was, I'd been secretly hoping we wouldn't have another trip out for a little while. We'd been to King Percival's before, so I knew that bit would be all right – but I wasn't at all sure if I liked the idea of a merry-go-round. I'd never been

15

on one, and I was certain I'd do something silly, like getting dizzy and falling off. For a moment I wondered if I could pretend to be ill the next day – but then I remembered I was trying to be a Perfect Princess, and earn enough tiara points to win my Silver Sash, and a place at Ruby Mansions.

"Perfect Princesses," I told myself firmly, "don't tell lies! And they try to be BRAVE!"

Sophia was still looking at the invitation on the board.

"It doesn't tell us what to wear," she said. "Do we have to dress as flowers for a Flower Petal Ball?"

Princess Diamonde and her twin sister, Gruella, heard her, and Diamonde sniggered.

"Sophia could go as a dandelion, couldn't she, Gruella?"

"ALL the Silver Rose Roomers could go as weeds!" Gruella said, and the two of them collapsed in a fit of giggles.

Sophia TOTALLY ignored them, and took my arm. "Shall we go and ask Fairy Angora?"

I nodded. Fairy Angora is the fairy godmother at Silver Towers, and she was sure to know.

"FANCY! Sophia's actually had a good idea!" Diamonde said loudly. "Gruella – why don't we see Fairy Angora at break time?" And she flounced away.

"Quick!" Katie said. "Let's go right now!"

The six of us hurried along the corridor, and knocked at Fairy Angora's door.

"DO come in!" Fairy Angora has the loveliest tinkling voice. "Door – OPEN!"

The door turned a glowing pink, but it stayed shut. Sometimes Fairy Angora's magic just doesn't work.

Alice grinned and turned the handle, and we trooped inside.

Fairy Angora was sitting at her desk, which had a vase of gorgeous apple blossom on it.

"What can I do for you, my darlings?" she asked.

"Please," Sophia said, "we're not sure what to wear tomorrow."

"Wear your prettiest summer dresses, angels!" Fairy Angora said. "Something fresh and flowery – that'll be perfect for the fair AND the Flower Petal Ball."

We looked at each other anxiously. NONE of us had flowery dresses.

"Don't worry, darlings!" Fairy Angora had seen our faces. "Pop in here after lessons with what you've got." She waved at her vase. "I've been practising a little flowery magic, so we'll see what I can do! But don't be late, my angels. I've got a meeting with King Percival, and I mustn't keep him waiting!"

Chapter Two

Of course we felt MUCH better after seeing Fairy Angora. In fact, we didn't really concentrate all that day because we were so busy wondering what our dresses would look like...which wasn't a good idea at all.

Queen Mother Matilda gave us two minus points each for

whispering during our lesson in the Gracious Acceptance of Royal Bouquets, and then Crown Prince Dandino told me off for not paying attention when he was showing us how to Step out of a Coach with Dignity and Poise.

"You must stay in for an extra half an hour after classes," he ordered, "and PRACTISE!"

I BEGGED him to let me go, but he wouldn't change his mind. Emily and Sophia pleaded with him too, and then he said we ALL had to stay...it was AWFUL!

As soon as he let us go we DASHED up to Silver Rose Room to collect our dresses, and then ZOOMED down to Fairy Angora's room. We lined up outside her door – and that's where Lady Albina saw us.

"May I ask exactly what you girls are doing?" she asked. She never sounds very friendly. Alice says her big sister reckons Lady Albina doesn't like anybody except Queen Samantha Joy.

"Please," Katie said, "we're here to see Fairy Angora."

"Well, you won't find her HERE," Lady Albina snapped. "She's having a very important meeting with King Percival, and she won't be free until the garden fair tomorrow."

As Lady Albina swept away we looked at each other blankly.

"No flowery dresses," Sophia said, and she sounded SO sad.

I felt COMPLETELY terrible. If ONLY I'd paid attention during Prince Dandino's lesson we'd have been in time to catch Fairy Angora.

Emily knew what I was thinking, and squeezed my hand. "At least we'll all be the same," she said. "Think how horrid it would be if half of us had fabulous flowery dresses and the others didn't!"

"That's right!" Alice was pretending to be cheerful. "Who

wants to look like a flowerbed, anyway?"

"YES!" Charlotte actually managed a smile. "Let's be different!"

I didn't say anything. I was trying hard not to cry.

*

We did our best to look summery for the Garden Fair. Alice and Katie both had gingham check dresses, and Sophia's was white with a little pink stripe.

Emily's dress had blue spots, and Charlotte and I were both wearing pink.

They were pretty dresses, but when we saw what the other princesses were wearing we did feel VERY ordinary.

"OOOOOH!" Diamonde trilled when she saw us. "It's the WEEDS!" She twirled round so we could see the lovely twirls of honeysuckle on her rustling silk skirts.

"OUR mother ALWAYS makes sure we have dresses for EVERY occasion!" Gruella told us, and she and Diamonde smirked at each other.

Gruella's dress was sprinkled with the sweetest little primroses, and there were more primroses on her tiara. I couldn't help thinking that even though she's not always very nice, she did look GORGEOUS.

"Everybody ready?" Crown Prince Dandino was waiting at

the door. "Hop in the coaches, and we'll be off!"

We hung back a little as the coaches filled with chattering princesses.

"We can still have fun," Emily said bravely.

"That's right." Sophia suddenly sat up, and smiled. "I'm sure Perfect Princesses don't mind WHAT they wear!"

"Of course they don't," Katie said firmly.

"Diamonde will have to be REALLY careful of her dress," Charlotte pointed out. "She was tripping over it just getting into the coach!"

Alice grinned. "Let's go on the merry-go-round as soon as we get there! Agreed?"

Everyone shouted "YES!"...and I did too, although I had a wobbly feeling in my stomach.

Just in case anyone noticed, I said,
"Is it all right if we go for a boat
ride on the lake straight
afterwards? I LOVE boats!"

"Fine by me!" Alice said
cheerfully, but I saw Sophia and
Emily look at each other.

"What's wrong?" I asked.

"Erm…" Emily said, and she was blushing. "I'm really REALLY sorry – but I don't like the water very much. I'm HOPELESS at swimming!"

"It's HORRID being scared of things," Sophia said. "You mustn't worry, Emily – I'm always terrified if I think I can't put my feet on the bottom!"

Chapter Three

I looked at my friends, and felt SO much better…but I also felt a little bit mean. They'd been brave enough to say they were scared, and I hadn't.

"Actually," I said, "can I tell you something?"

They looked at me in surprise.

"Can't you swim either, Daisy?"

asked Katie.

"It's not that," I said, "it's the merry-go-round. It makes my legs go wobbly every time I think about it!"

There was a second's silence, and then we all began to laugh. It was as if a HUGE weight had fallen off me, and I think Emily and Sophia felt a little bit the same.

"Right!" Alice said. "We'll ALL look after each other! First we'll try the merry-go-round, and then the boating lake – and if anyone wants to sit and watch that's TOTALLY OK!"

And we solemnly shook hands.

We were much the last to arrive at King Percival's palace. The coach we were supposed to travel in had a loose wheel, and we had to wait while Prince Dandino organised another one. It was SO frustrating!

By the time we finally got there we were absolutely BURSTING with excitement, even if we weren't wearing flowery dresses. We totally tumbled out of the coach (it was a good thing Prince Dandino didn't see us!) and stared round.

King Percival's gardens looked BEAUTIFUL. Silver balloons were tied on every bush and tree, and they looked SO pretty as they shone in the sunshine! But the princesses and princes and queens and kings who were wandering around didn't look as if they were having a particularly wonderful time. We saw Princess Lisa and Princess Jemima, and they were sitting at the edge of the lake looking so BORED!

"What's the matter?" I asked. "Aren't you having fun?"

Princess Lisa shook her head. "There's nothing much to do.

The brass band hasn't turned up, the merry-go-round isn't working properly, and there are only two boats on the lake, and Princess Eglantine and Princess Nancy have been hogging them for AGES! We're just hanging about waiting for the Flower Petal Ball."

"Oh dear," I said, but Alice pulled at my arm.

"I can see the merry-go-round!" she said, her eyes sparkling. "Let's have a look at it!"

Emily held one of my hands as
we walked across the grass, and
Sophia the other. As we got closer,
I could see the merry-go-round did
look AMAZING.

It had the prettiest little coaches and carriages pulled by the sweetest silver ponies – and there, standing right in front of it, was Fairy Angora. She was deep in conversation with King Percival, who was looking very gloomy.

"Maybe we could ask her about our dresses!" Sophia whispered.

"She looks too busy at the moment," Alice said. "Why don't we try to have a go on the merry-go-round?"

"DO let's!" Emily said. 'Daisy can share with me, and then she'll be fine! OK, Daisy?"

I nodded, and I was just stepping into a sweet little carriage when Diamonde and Gruella appeared.

"Oh!" Gruella almost smiled. "That looks FUN!" She climbed in and sat beside me before I could say anything.

Diamonde frowned. "Gruella! Merry-go-rounds are for babies!" she sniffed, but she pushed me to one side so she could squash in too.

Emily made a sympathetic face at me, and sat down in the carriage next to mine. "Will you be all right?" she asked.

"OOOOH! Is poor little Daisy scared?" Diamonde asked.

I smoothed my skirts, and tried to look calm. "I'm QUITE all right," I said – and I SO hoped it was true!

The merry-go-round began to turn, but it went SO slowly. I kept thinking it was about to speed up, but it didn't. It lurched and shuddered as if it was about to stop any second, and it squeaked terribly.

King Percival and Fairy Angora looked up just as my carriage drew level with them.

"Oh NO!" King Percival groaned. "Still going slow, what? TYPICAL!"

"Everything's going wrong." He glared at Fairy Angora. "That's the trouble with magic! You can't rely on it! I'm going to find the Royal Engineer!" He stamped away across the grass.

Fairy Angora was looking very flustered. "POOR King Percival," she said. "Even the Royal Brass Band hasn't arrived yet."

"Couldn't you use your wand to

make things better?" I asked.

Fairy Angora hesitated. "I have been helping, my angel," she said. "I was here yesterday for AGES, sorting things out." She sighed. "Sometimes I think my magic isn't very good."

I felt SO sorry for her. "It wouldn't take much magic to make the merry-go-round work, would it?"

Diamonde sat back, folded her arms and sneered. "Silly Daisy! She means she CAN'T make it work!"

Chapter Four

I was so shocked! I couldn't believe she'd been so rude. Fairy Angora went BRIGHT PINK, and looked really angry.

"Princess Diamonde," she said, "take TEN minus tiara points, and come and see me in my office tomorrow!" She tapped our silver pony on its nose. "And for

your information, young lady,
I certainly CAN make this
merry-go-round work!"

There was a flash, a shower of
stars...and our silver pony
neighed, shook its head, and
charged off the merry-go-round

with our carriage rattling behind it – and at once all the other ponies followed!

I hung on tightly as we bumped and bounced over the grass. Diamonde and Gruella screamed and screamed and SCREAMED.

On either side princesses shrieked and ran, and I could see Lady Albina staring at us with her mouth wide open.

The ponies swerved round a flowerbed, and dashed straight

for the lake. They zoomed up to the edge, and hurled themselves in. As they swam out towards the middle of the lake, there was a shower of silver stars – and they VANISHED!

It was SO strange. Suddenly, we were floating peacefully on the water. Diamonde was still screaming, and Gruella was wailing that they were going to be drowned, but it really did feel safe.

I could see crowds gathering at the edge of the lake, and poor King Percival wiping his forehead and trying to calm everyone down, but I didn't feel scared at all. But then I remembered Emily and Sophia, and I turned to look at them. Their coaches were floating behind mine, and they were smiling at me, although I did think they looked rather pale.

Alice and Katie and Charlotte were grinning from ear to ear, so I knew they were fine. I peered out of our carriage, and it rocked wildly. Diamonde and Gruella screeched, but I didn't take any notice. The water was very clear and clean, and it didn't look deep.

In fact, it didn't look very deep at all...

I took my shoes off.

"Daisy's going to leave us here to DROOOOOOOOWN!" Gruella moaned.

"Oh no! I want MUMMY!" Diamonde howled.

I stepped out of the carriage, and the water only just reached the hem of my dress. "Come on," I said to Gruella and Diamonde. "I'll hold your hands."

As we all reached the shore there was a loud cheer, and King Percival stepped forward to help us onto the bank.

"Well done, young Daisy," he said. "Sorry about that. Was almost sure something would go wrong. Shouldn't have tried to mess with magic, I—"

But at that moment Queen Samantha Joy came sailing through the crowd, with Fairy Angora close behind her.

"I THINK," Queen Samantha Joy said, and her voice was shaking because she was so angry, "we need a very good EXPLANATION, King Percival! There seems to be something EXTREMELY unusual about your merry-go-round!"

If it hadn't been so awful, it would have been funny. King Percival looked like a naughty boy who'd been caught stealing apples. He hung his head, and shuffled his feet – and that was when I stepped forward.

Chapter Five

"Excuse me, Your Majesty, I said, and I curtsied as low as I could, "it's not King Percival's fault. It was me—" I stopped to swallow hard. 'You see, I suggested that Fairy Angora used magic on the merry-go-round. I'm TRULY sorry—" but I had to stop.

Fairy Angora was waving her

wand at me. "It wasn't Princess Daisy's fault at all," she said. "It was MINE—"

"HARRUMPH!" King Percival made the LOUDEST snorting noise. "Nothing of the kind! ALL my fault! Wanted to have a good day, d'you see – persuaded Fairy Angora to do me a favour. Had her making magic all yesterday, you see – got her to turn my carriage ponies into merry-go-round ponies. Stupid, really. Should have known I'd mess up. Humble apologies, Your Majesty. Won't happen again!"

"I see." Queen Samantha Joy's

voice was shaking so much I couldn't help staring at her – and now she seemed to be LAUGHING! "Well, King Percival, I have to tell you that I usually find garden fairs a touch on the boring side – but I shall ALWAYS remember this one!"

"But WE didn't think it was funny!" Diamonde said, glaring.

"That's right!" Gruella said. "We nearly DROWNED!"

Fairy Angora whispered something to Queen Samantha

Joy. Our headteacher looked at Diamonde, and she was suddenly VERY serious.

"If I am correct, Princess Diamonde, it was YOU that made Fairy Angora so angry she forgot to behave in a suitably responsible manner. There is a coach waiting at the entrance to the garden, and I suggest you and your sister go STRAIGHT back to Silver Towers to think about your attitude. The rest of us will continue enjoying the fair. King Percival, do I hear your brass band? They must have arrived after all!"

Queen Samantha Joy tucked her
arm into King Percival's, and
walked him away. She had almost
disappeared into the crowd when
she turned, and called, "Fairy
Angora! DO see those poor girls
don't catch their death of cold!"

Fairy Angora was standing
staring at the lake, a puzzled look
on her face. When she heard
Queen Samantha Joy, she jumped.

"Oh! You poor little darlings!"
She looked at our damp dresses.
"Oh oh OH! I remember now. You
were going to come and see me
yesterday about your dresses, but
I had to rush off and meet King

Percival! Oh, I'm so very VERY sorry! What a TERRIBLE time you've had." She pulled her wand out of her bag, and blew on the end of it. "Now...let me see...can I get this right, do you think?"

She twirled her wand in the air – and we GASPED. Our dresses were totally AMAZING! It was as if they'd been made from a froth of pink and white apple blossom, with shimmery pink petticoats. They were the most GORGEOUS dresses I'd ever seen – and we had glittery pink shoes to match!

"THANK YOU!" we chorused. "Thank you VERY MUCH!"

Fairy Angora beamed. "They have turned out well, haven't they?" she said.

"Now, if I could only work out what happened to those ponies…"

"LOOK!" It was Katie, and she was pointing at the lake. "THERE they are! They're trotting out of the water...and they're not even wet!" She rubbed her eyes. "But they're not silver any more. They're REAL!"

"Of course they are," Fairy Angora said, sounding very relieved. "And I'm SO pleased to see them! I couldn't think WHAT I was going to say to King Percival if they'd really gone for good. Now, are you going to help

me catch them? Maybe you'd like to ride them across to the crystal tower. It must almost be time for the Flower Petal Ball!"

Of course we were thrilled...and as we rode round the palace ground and up to the crystal tower we felt like the most Perfect Princesses in the whole wide world.

Chapter Six

Have you ever been to a Flower Petal Ball? It was SO magic. You couldn't see the walls for the garlands of flowers, and as we danced, petals drifted in the air. The scent of roses and lavender and honeysuckle was everywhere, and beautiful butterflies fluttered from blossom to blossom.

As the evening grew darker, silver stars floated up into the velvet night sky, and tiny twinkly lights shone in among the glossy ivy leaves that twisted round the tall stone pillars.

King Percival's Royal Orchestra played the SWEETEST music, and we danced until our feet were sore...and our gorgeous apple blossom dresses glimmered and shimmered in the twilight. It was absolutely HEAVENLY.

*

When we finally rolled home to Silver Towers I was SO tired. We hung our gorgeous dresses up, and whispered "Good night!" to each other as we crawled into bed.

"Thank you for a LOVELY time, Daisy," Emily said sleepily.

"Me?" I said, surprised. "I didn't do anything!"

"Yes you did." Katie yawned a huge yawn. "You made it a FUN day!"

"I didn't exactly mean to," I said. "Anyway, it was fun because we were there together…"

And I meant it. Friends are the best thing ever…and I'm SO glad you're our friend too.

The Tiara Club
at Silver Towers

Princess Alice
and the Crystal Slipper

By Vivian French
Illustrated by Sarah Gibb

ORCHARD BOOKS

Hi! How are you doing? It's so brilliant that you're here at Silver Towers - you're a real STAR. Not like the twins - Princess Diamonde and Princess Gruella. They're SO stuck-up and horrible. Sometimes I almost hope they won't get enough tiara points to win their Silver Sashes and go on to Ruby Mansions...but that's NOT the way a Perfect Princess ought to think!

Oh - I forgot to say. I'm Princess Alice and I share the Silver Rose Room with Charlotte, Katie, Daisy, Sophia and Emily. They're my best friends, and we try to do everything together...

Chapter One

Do you go on school outings? Ever since we've been at Silver Towers we've had one trip out after another. Our headteacher, Queen Samantha Joy, says that it's good for us – and they usually do end up being quite fun! But we were SERIOUSLY excited when Queen Samantha Joy told us we were going to go to King Rudolfo the Third's private Museum of Royal Life. My big sis went there when she was at Silver Towers (she's at Ruby Mansions now) and she said it was AMAZING! She saw the Poisoned Apple, and the Crystal Slipper, and the Spinning Wheel – and loads of other really fantastic things.

Lady Albina (she's Queen Samantha Joy's secretary, and organises us with about fifty thousand lists every single day) heard me telling my friends about the museum after morning assembly was over, and frowned at me. She's always frowning, unless she's talking to Queen Samantha Joy.

"Princess Alice, I do hope you don't think you know everything already!" she snapped.

I heard Princess Diamonde snigger, and whisper, "SHE doesn't, but WE do, don't we?" to Gruella, but I pretended I hadn't heard.

"Oh no! I really don't," I said, and curtsied to Lady Albina.

"I'm glad to hear it! That is how mistakes are made! Tomorrow you will be divided into groups. Each group will have a questionnaire to complete, and tiara points will be awarded for the best entries. And—" Lady Albina looked even more disapproving – "King Rudolfo has offered a prize. A QUITE unnecessary kindness, if you ask me."

"A PRIZE?" We clustered round Lady Albina. Even Diamonde and Gruella looked excited. "Please, Lady Albina – WHAT prize?"

Lady Albina sniffed. "The winning group will be invited to take part in King Rudolfo's Annual Royal Parade. They will, I understand, ride in the Golden Pumpkin Coach."

A royal parade! And a golden pumpkin coach! It sounded SO wonderful. We couldn't help talking about it every time we had a spare moment in between lessons, and that night we were MUCH too excited to sleep.

"We will be in the same group, won't we?" Daisy asked. It would be SO awful if we weren't."

"Of course we will be," Emily

said comfortingly. "Lady Albina chooses by dormitories."

"Hurrah! for the Silver Rose Roomers!" Katie cheered. "And you know all about the museum, Alice – so we'll have a really good chance of winning."

I shook my head. "I only know what my big sis said."

"Is everything in glass cases?" Charlotte asked. "Or can we touch them?"

"NO!' Sophia looked horrified. "Imagine touching a poisoned apple!"

Emily giggled. "We'd all fall over and look as if we were dead, and have to wait to be kissed by a handsome—"

She was interrupted by a knock on the door, and Fairy Angora appeared. She's our school Fairy Godmother, and she keeps an eye on us all.

"Too much noise, my precious darlings," she said. "It's time to go to sleep!"

She waved her wand, and a drift of twinkly sparkles floated into the air...and I suddenly couldn't keep my eyes open a second longer.

Chapter Two

I had the weirdest dream! I was wearing a pair of absolutely gorgeous crystal slippers, and I was dancing all by myself in the middle of a huge ballroom...and then I felt someone shaking me.

"Alice! Wake up! Come on!" It was Charlotte. "The bell's gone – you've got to get up! It's the visit to the museum today – we've got to hurry!"

I forgot all about my dream, and ZOOMED out of bed.

Lady Albina fussed about giving out questionnaires and pencils

and instructions all the time we were eating our breakfast. Honestly – it almost made me not want to go! Luckily Crown Prince Dandino came bouncing into the breakfast hall just as we finished. He organises our school outings,

and he's good fun.

"Everyone ready for a fabulous day out?" he asked. "We'll be going to King Rudolfo's library first, to see some of his books. Then we'll visit the museum, and you can have a good look at the exhibits, and at the end of the morning we'll meet up back in the library. You can finish filling in your questionnaires while you're there. Lunch will be in the state dining room, and afterwards you can wander round the gardens while King Rudolfo and I look at your work. We'll announce the tiara points awarded and the winners of the competition at a little ceremony before we all go home!"

I was really glad when we finally rolled up the enormous drive to King Rudolfo's palace. All of us Silver Rose Roomers were in the same coach, and so were Princess Jemima, Princess Lisa, Princess

Freya and Princess Chloe.
Unfortunately the twins were
there as well – and Diamonde
spent the whole journey telling us
how she and Gruella had been to
the museum before.

"Of course," Diamonde
boasted, "we had tea with King
Rudy, didn't we, Gruella?"

Gruella nodded enthusiastically.
"King Rudy gave us FIFTEEN
different kinds of cake."

"I thought he was called King
Rudolfo," Emily said.

"He is, but his special friends
call him King Rudy, and
Mummy's one of his MOST

special friends." Diamonde looked SO pleased with herself as she sat back, almost as if she was expecting a round of applause.

"That's nice," Daisy said, but she didn't sound very impressed. Diamonde leant forward, and

went on boasting.

"AND he let us hold the pea that was under the mattresses, and look in the magic mirror, and do whatever we wanted. Didn't he, Gruella?"

Gruella nodded again, but it was odd. She was suddenly

looking a bit uncomfortable.

Diamonde coughed loudly. "AHEM! And do you know what else? King Rudy even let me try on the crystal slipper!"

"Goodness!" said Princess Chloe, and her eyes were very big and round. "Did he really?"

Diamonde smiled a self-satisfied smile. "It fitted me PERFECTLY."

I hadn't been paying her much attention, because I was wondering what was wrong with Gruella, but that made me sit up.

"You can't have worn the slipper," I said, surprised. "I SO want to try it, but my big sis told me nobody's EVER allowed to!"

Diamonde went bright red, and glared at me. "Well, I did! Didn't I, Gruella?" And I was sure I saw her pinch her twin.

"Oh – yes," Gruella said, and nodded hard.

"You'll see!" Diamonde hissed at me. "Just because you've got a big sister doesn't mean you know everything!"

I didn't answer. I was almost certain Diamonde had been telling fibs, and when I looked at my friends' faces I knew they thought so too.

Chapter Three

As soon as the coach stopped, Diamonde grabbed Gruella, and the two of them pushed their way out before the rest of us had even picked up our bags.

An incredibly tall, thin king wearing horn-rimmed spectacles was leaning against the wall, and Diamonde positively elbowed

Prince Dandino out of the way as she dashed towards him.

"King Rudy!" she squealed, and sank into a curtsey. "Mummy says she's just LONGING to see you again!"

A nasty little bit of me was hoping King Rudolfo would say,

"WHO? WHAT? Who are you?" but he didn't. He smiled a rather absent-minded smile, and said, "Many thanks, my dear – many thanks indeed." He took off his spectacles, cleaned them, then put them back on and peered at the rest of us.

"Welcome to you all," he said. "We'll start in the library, shall we?"

Number one on our questionnaire was, *"How many books are there in King Rudolfo's library?"*, and I was very glad we didn't have to count them, because there were thousands! He told us there were about fifty thousand, but he couldn't be certain.

"Excuse me, Your Majesty," I said, "but might I ask how many you've read?"

Diamonde gave a little shriek. "Oh! Alice! You can't mean your super special big sister didn't tell you? King Rudy's got MUCH more important things to do than read books – haven't you, King Rudy?"

King Rudolfo looked at Diamonde in a puzzled sort of way.

"Actually, my dear," he said, "I think reading is a totally delightful occupation. There isn't much you can't learn from a book. Now, shall I let you all have a wander round? My housekeeper will bring you something to drink very shortly." And he patted Diamonde on the head as he wandered away.

Diamonde looked cross for a moment, then waved her arm at the books as if they belonged to her.

"Shall I show you round?" she said. "After all, Gruella and I have been here before."

"No thank you," I said. "We'll look for ourselves." And I'm sorry if that sounded rude, but I was getting SO fed up with Diamonde being such a show-off.

"Oooooh," Diamonde sneered. "Guess who thinks her big sister has told her everything there is to know!"

I didn't answer. I took Charlotte's arm, and we went to look at a row of pictures of King Rudolfo's family. Daisy, Emily, Katie and Sophia came with us, and we studied the huge paintings carefully.

"Look!" Daisy said. "All King Rudolfo's relations are holding books!"

Katie chuckled. "So that's question number two answered. *How do King Rudolfo's family entertain themselves when they are at leisure?*"

"I do wish we could go to the museum," I said. "I'm dying to see the crystal slipper!"

And, just as if she'd heard me, at that moment the housekeeper came in with a tray of juice and biscuits.

"I've just opened the museum,' she announced as she put the tray down. "King Rudolfo says he'll be back in twenty minutes or so to show you round."

"Must we wait for him?"
I asked.

The housekeeper smiled at me.

"You can wait for him in the museum if you've finished here. It's just down the corridor and through the swing doors."

We looked at each other.

"Do you want a drink?" I asked. "Or shall we go now?"

"Let's go now!" Emily said, and Sophia, Daisy, Katie and Charlotte nodded.

The museum wasn't very big, but it was absolutely crammed with glass cases, and the walls had shelves reaching right up to the ceiling. It was quite scary; the shelves were piled so high with papers and boxes and bits and pieces I couldn't help thinking we'd be totally buried if they fell down. It felt more like a workroom or a study than a museum, and we found ourselves whispering as we tiptoed round.

"Wow!" Charlotte was staring into a little silver casket. "Here's a pea! It says it's the actual pea the princess felt under all the mattresses!"

Sophia came to look. "It looks very shrivelled," she said doubtfully.

Katie pointed to a corner. "That looks like the spinning wheel!"

We went to look, and she was quite right. Beside it was a

tottering heap of pure gold plates, all with the most complicated royal crests.

"It says these came from Cinderella's wedding," Daisy whispered as she read the label.

"There's half an apple on that shelf," Katie whispered back. "Do you—"

She stopped, because Diamonde and Gruella were standing in the doorway...and there was something very sneaky about the way they were looking round.

We didn't mean to spy on them. We really really didn't – although I suppose if we'd been truly Perfect Princesses we'd have stepped forward as soon as we saw them and said hello. As it was, we stayed in our dark corner and watched to see what they were up to.

"King Rudy won't be here for at LEAST ten minutes," Diamonde said. "We've got LOADS of time." And she put up her hand and switched on the light.

It made SUCH a difference! There was a magnificent chandelier in the middle of the room, and it glittered and shone, and sent sparkles of light flashing over the glass cases. In particular it lit up a tall case that was immediately beneath, and I don't know why Diamonde and Gruella didn't hear us as we ooohed and

aaaahed. The crystal slipper was SO gorgeous – I don't know how we could possibly have missed it when we first came in.

I was just moving out of our dark corner when Katie pulled me back.

"Look at Diamonde!" she
hissed in my ear. I looked, and my
mouth dropped WIDE open.

Diamonde was trying to lift up
the glass cover over the crystal
slipper!

"Here!" she snapped at Gruella.
"Can't you see I need help?"

Gruella didn't look at all happy.
"I don't think—" she began, but
Diamonde took no notice.

"I told Chloe I'd worn the
crystal slipper," she said, "and
I'm going to wear it – so
THERE!"

She gave the glass cover one
last heave, lifted it off – and

DROPPED IT!

Splinters of glass flew everywhere, and the CRASH! was tremendous. Daisy screamed, and Emily shrieked, and Charlotte, Sophia, Katie and I gasped as we hurried out from behind the cases. At once Diamonde snatched up

the slipper, and pushed it into my hands. When Prince Dandino and King Rudolfo came hurrying in a second later, followed by all the Silver Towers princesses, there I was – standing in the middle of a heap of shattered glass, and clutching the crystal slipper.

As everyone stared and stared and STARED at me Diamonde said, "She told us she'd always wanted to try on the slipper. We all heard her, didn't we Chloe?"

What could poor Chloe say? She went bright red, and nodded. Prince Dandino folded his arms, and frowned at me.

"I can't say how disappointed I am, Princess Alice. I've always thought of you as one of our star pupils, but this is a terrible TERRIBLE thing to have done!"

I didn't know what to do. I couldn't say it was Diamonde who had broken the glass case, because that would have been telling tales – and I knew my friends would feel exactly the same. I stared down at the crystal slipper, and I was so muddled and angry and embarrassed I began to blush.

"See?" Diamonde sounded triumphant. "She's going all red!"

"Princess Alice – I think you'd better go straight to the library," Prince Dandino said sternly. "And when we get back to Silver Towers we'll see what Queen Samantha Joy has to say."

"Yes, Your Highness," I said, and I was about to curtsey when I remembered I was still holding the crystal slipper. I held it out to King Rudolfo.

"Please excuse me, Your Majesty," I said. "And I am very VERY sorry that this has happened."

King Rudolfo took the slipper, and then he did SUCH an odd

thing. He gave me a little bow, and said, "Before you retire to the library, Princess Alice, would you like to try on the crystal slipper?"

I couldn't believe my ears. I was SO unprincessy! I really and truly gawped at him. Prince Dandino made a tut-tutting noise.

"I don't think Princess Alice deserves such an honour, Your Majesty," he said.

King Rudolfo gave a funny little smile, and said, "Please allow this, Prince Dandino. I have my reasons."

So I took off my shoe, and King Rudolfo slid the slipper onto my foot!

It was WEIRD. It fitted quite well, but it was a little bit tight round my heel – and it felt so cold and hard.

I couldn't imagine how anybody could have danced in a pair of crystal slippers. It only goes to show how very special the real owner must have been.

"Thank you," King Rudolfo said as he gently took the slipper off again. "And now, would anyone else like to try?"

Of   course   just   about

EVERYONE put their hands up. King Rudolfo beckoned to Diamonde.

"Why don't you try, Princess... oh, I'm so sorry." He shook his head. "I've forgotten your name."

Diamonde pouted, then smiled a forgiving smile. "I'm Queen Euphemia's daughter," she reminded him. "I'm Princess Diamonde. And I'd LOVE to try on the crystal slipper!"

And that was when I had a BRILLIANT idea. I wasn't going to tell on Diamonde – but I WAS going to make sure she didn't get away with everything.

I swept King Rudolfo my very best curtsey, and I said, "Thank you for your kindness, King Rudolfo. It was most generous of you, and I have no right to ask anything of you – but as Princess Diamonde has already tried the slipper, might another princess have the honour, perhaps?"

King Rudolfo raised his eyebrows. "Princess Diamonde has already tried the slipper?"

If looks could kill, I'd have been flat on the floor. Diamonde GLARED at me as she said, "But I haven't, Your Majesty. Princess Alice must be mistaken."

"No she isn't!" It was little Princess Chloe. "You told us you did, Diamonde! When we were in the coach, remember? You said King Rudy had let you try on the slipper, and it fitted you perfectly!"

There was a long pause. It was SO obvious that Diamonde had been telling fibs. She went absolutely PURPLE, and shuffled her feet, and muttered about only pretending, and she hadn't really meant it.

King Rudolfo stroked his chin thoughtfully as he listened. Then he held the slipper out.

"Please put it on," he commanded.

Diamonde gulped. She took

the slipper, put it on – and immediately began to hop and skip all over the broken glass.

"HELP!" she squealed. "HELP! I can't STOP!" But it was no good. Round and round the glass cases she danced, spinning in circles.

"Princess Diamonde! STOP THIS MINUTE!" Prince Dandino roared, but it was no good. Poor Diamonde couldn't stop. King Rudolfo was frowning, but most of the Silver Towers princesses were laughing and laughing and LAUGHING. She did look funny – but it was horrible as well because she looked SO unhappy.

I ran to her, and took her hand.

"I'll help you," I said. "Hang on to me – try and kick the slipper off!"

But Diamonde couldn't. The next thing I knew I was hopping and skipping as well, and when

Charlotte grabbed me she began dancing too.

King Rudolfo held up his hand.

"I think," he said, "Princess Diamonde has something to say."

And Diamonde, puffing hard and bright red with her hair all over her face, panted, "It was ME! I broke the glass case! I'm very very sorry..."

She stopped at once, and

flopped against me. Charlotte and I almost had to hold her up.

Prince Dandino strode across the room looking REALLY angry, but I moved in front of Diamonde. I couldn't help it.

I knew she was a show-off and told boastful fibs, but I also knew how AWFUL it must have been having everyone laughing, and not being able to stop.

"Please," I said, "please don't be too cross with her. She didn't mean to break the glass, really she didn't."

King Rudolfo nodded.

"Princess Alice is quite right," he said. "Princess Diamonde has had punishment enough." He took my hand and kissed it.

"It's a delight to meet such a Perfect Princess."

"Me?" I said in surprise.

"A true princess never laughs at the misfortunes of others... however well deserved those misfortunes may be." For a second I thought I saw a tiny twinkle in his eye – but I might have been wrong. Then he went on.

"I suggest that Princess Alice's generosity is rewarded. Shall we forget the questionnaire, Prince Dandino, and ask Princess Alice and her friends to lead my Royal Parade tomorrow, and to ride in the Golden Pumpkin Coach?"

Chapter Six

So that was how Charlotte, Katie, Daisy, Sophia, Emily and I spent the next day...and it was GLORIOUS! We spent the whole morning getting ready (we were wearing our very best dresses), and then at exactly twelve o'clock the Golden Pumpkin Coach came rolling up to Silver Towers, pulled by six gorgeous golden ponies. We settled ourselves inside, and then off we went...all the way

round the town, with the rest of
the Royal Parade marching and
dancing and singing behind us.

There were THOUSANDS of people watching, and we bowed and smiled until our faces were sore. And at the end of the day we went back to King Rudolfo's palace, and – guess what!

Yes – we had the most amazing tea, and there were THIRTY different kinds of cake. Charlotte and I counted them.

And just before we were finally driven back to Silver Towers the housekeeper gave us the left over cakes to share with all our other friends...

When it was bedtime, I found Diamonde waiting for me by Silver Rose Room door. She looked really awkward and embarrassed.

"Sorry," she mumbled – and then she was off down the stairs as fast as she could go.

And as I snuggled down in my bed, I thought how wonderful life was at Silver Towers...and I'm SO glad you're here with us.

Here's a taster of the next book!

ISBN 978 1 40830 677 2

£4.99

Hello! I'm Princess Sophia,
and I'm a Tiara Club princess
here at Silver Towers - just like you!
And I'm SO glad you're here with us.
I expect you know my friends who share
Silver Rose Room with me. There's Alice,
and Daisy, and Katie and Charlotte and
Emily - and I just KNOW that if we
get enough Tiara Points to win our
Silver Sashes, and go on to Ruby Towers,
we'll still be the very best friends ever.
We're not too friendly with Princess
Diamonde and her twin sister Gruella,
though. They just LOVE showing off,
and being mean...

Chapter One

It was Wednesday, and we were late getting up. Katie was still in her pyjamas and Alice was only half-dressed when the last bell rang for breakfast. Charlotte dropped her hairbrush, and looked horrified.

"Oh NO!" she said. "Lady Albina's going to be FURIOUS!

We'll get about a million minus tiara points!"

Lady Albina is the school secretary, and she's usually floating about at breakfast time. She only smiles when Queen Samantha Joy is around, and she's always telling us off for not being Perfect Princesses – and handing out minus tiara points.

Emily groaned. "I've already got three this week," she said. "I forgot to hand in my Ideal Banquet Arrangements to Lady Victoria, and she was in a bad mood."

"But we did get five points each for knowing how to flutter a fan while curtseying," I said.

"You mean YOU did," Katie said as she scrambled into her dress. "I only got two."

Daisy sighed. "And me."

"Never mind about fans," Charlotte interrupted. "Just let's GO!"

We hurried down the stairs, hoping we might be able to sneak in without being seen...

But Lady Albina was standing outside the dining hall pinning a notice on the board. She frowned at us as we sank into our most apologetic curtsies.

"I'm SO sorry we're late, Lady Albina," I said.

Lady Albina looked at her watch in a meaningful way. "You are VERY LATE INDEED, Princess Sophia," she snapped. "Such behaviour is intolerable! Please report to Queen Samantha Joy immediately after breakfast, and I will not be at all surprised if she forbids you to attend Prince Maurice's party!" Then she sniffed loudy, and stalked away with her nose in the air.

We stared at each other. Finally Emily said, "Who's Prince Maurice? And why would he ask us to his party?"

Alice shook her head. "I don't

know. My big sister's never said anything about a Prince Maurice."

Charlotte sighed. "I do hope we can go. It's AGES since we've been to a party."

Daisy was looking worried. "Do you think Queen Samantha Joy will be VERY angry with us?"

"We'd better have breakfast and find out," Katie said, and we followed her into the dining hall.

Of course the only places left were next to the terrible twins, Diamonde and Gruella, and Diamonde looked SO superior as we sat down.

"Don't any of you know that

Perfect Princesses are meant to be on time for their appointments?" she asked.

We ignored her, and Emily turned to Gruella. "Do you know anything about a party?" she asked. "Prince Maurice's party?"

Gruella shook her head, but Diamonde snorted.

"Typical," she sneered. "Trust one of the Silver Rose Roomers to pretend she knows something before the rest of us!"

Emily went very pink, and bit her lip. I jumped up and glared at Diamonde.

"That's SO unfair!" I said. "Lady Albina told us!" As I spoke, I suddenly remembered. Lady Albina had been pinning up a notice when we saw her. I was so sure it was about the party that I went to check...and walked straight into our headteacher, Queen Samantha Joy.

Enjoy more fabulous Tiara Club adventures!

ISBN 978 1 40830 582 9

£4.99

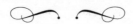

Two stories in one – plus stickers!

The Tiara Club

Daisy & Alice
at the
Princess Academy

Vivian French Illustrated by Sarah Gibb

ISBN 978 1 40830 583 6

£4.99

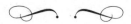

Two stories in one – plus stickers!

The Tiara Club

Sophia & Emily
at the
Princess Academy

Vivian French   Illustrated by Sarah Gibb

ISBN 978 1 40830 584 3

£4.99

ISBN 978 1 40830 675 8

£4.99

Have you read the Tiara Club at Ruby Mansions?

ISBN 978 1 84616 290 9

£3.99

ISBN 978 1 84616 291 6

£3.99

ISBN 978 1 84616 292 3

£3.99

ISBN 978 1 84616 293 0

£3.99

ISBN 978 1 84616 294 7

£3.99

ISBN 978 1 84616 295 4

£3.99

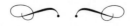

Have you read the Tiara Club
at Pearl Palace?

ISBN 978 1 84616 498 9

£3.99

ISBN 978 1 84616 499 6

£3.99

ISBN 978 1 84616 500 9

£3.99

ISBN 978 1 84616 501 6

£3.99

ISBN 978 1 84616 502 3

£3.99

ISBN 978 1 84616 503 0

£3.99

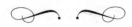

Have you read the Tiara Club at Emerald Castle?

ISBN 978 1 84616 869 7

£3.99

ISBN 978 1 84616 870 3

£3.99

ISBN 978 1 84616 871 0

£3.99

ISBN 978 1 84616 872 7

£3.99

ISBN 978 1 84616 873 4

£3.99

ISBN 978 1 84616 874 1

£3.99

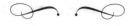

Have you read the Tiara Club at Diamond Turrets?

ISBN 978 1 84616 875 8

£3.99

ISBN 978 1 84616 876 5

£3.99

ISBN 978 1 84616 877 2

£3.99

ISBN 978 1 84616 878 9

£3.99

ISBN 978 1 84616 879 6

£3.99

ISBN 978 1 84616 880 2

£3.99

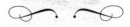

Have you read the Tiara Club specials?

ISBN 978 1 84616 470 5

£5.99

ISBN 978 1 84616 296 1

£5.99

ISBN 978 1 84616 504 7

£5.99

ISBN 978 1 84616 881 9

£5.99

ISBN 978 1 84616 882 6

£5.99

ISBN 978 1 40830 579 9

£5.99

ISBN 978 1 40830 580 5

£5.99

Don't miss **The Tiara Club** website at:

www.tiaraclub.co.uk

Keep up to date with the latest
Tiara Club books and meet all
your favourite princesses!

There is SO much to see and do,
including games and activities. You can
even become an exclusive member of the
Tiara Club Princess Academy.

PLUS, there's exciting
competitions with
WONDERFUL prizes!

Be a Perfect Princess – check it out today